I Will Hold You 'Til You Sleep

by

LINDA
ZUCKERMAN

illustrated by

JON J MUTH

Scholastic Press • Arthur A. Levine Books

IMPRINTS OF SCHOLASTIC INC.

I will hold you 'til you sleep
Safe and warm within my arms

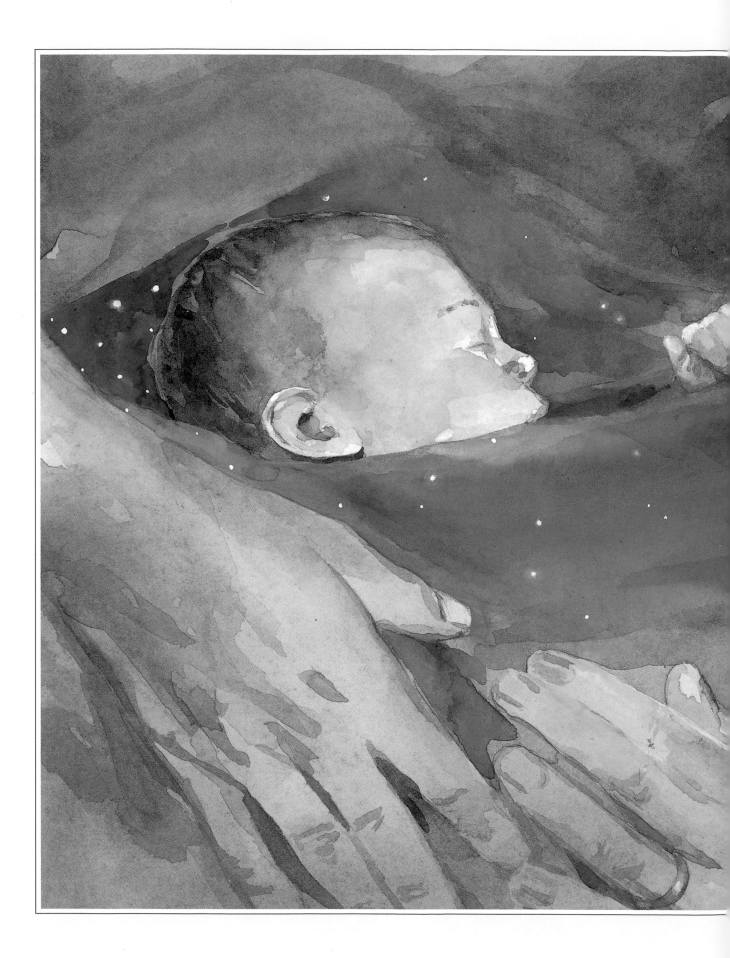

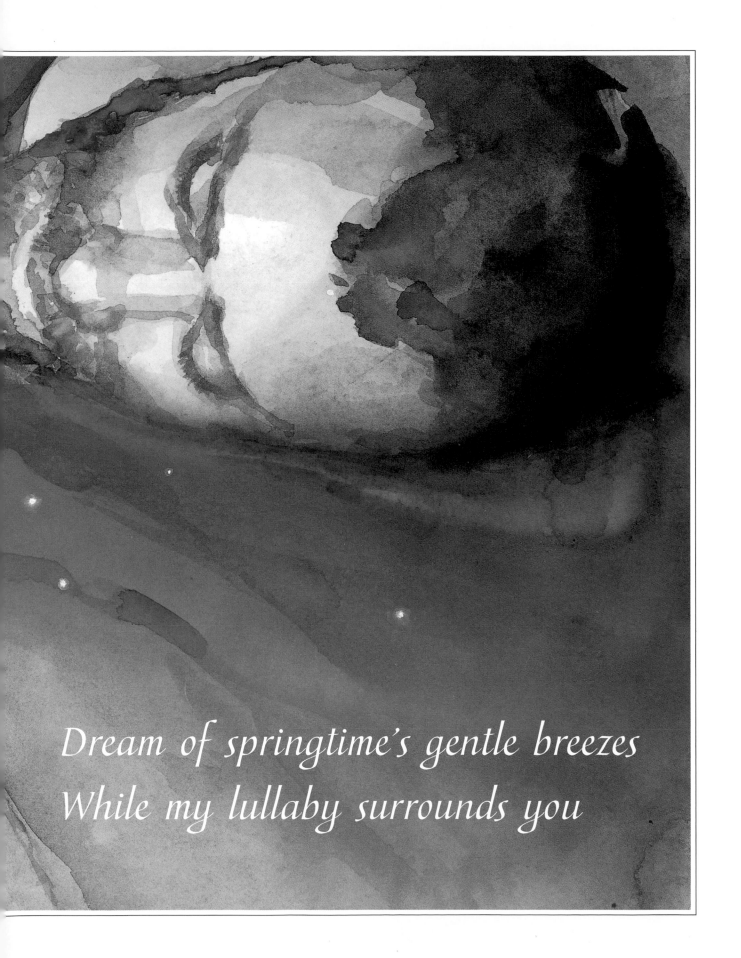

Dream of springtime's gentle breezes
While my lullaby surrounds you

Dearest baby, child of mine
I will hold you 'til you sleep.

I will hug you when you wake
Summer sun will fill your day

But if gray clouds storm and thunder
I'll be shelter from the rain

Dearest baby, child of mine

I will hug you when you wake.

*I will kiss you when you fall
Stumbling on a rocky path*

While the leaves of autumn fly
We will laugh the pain away

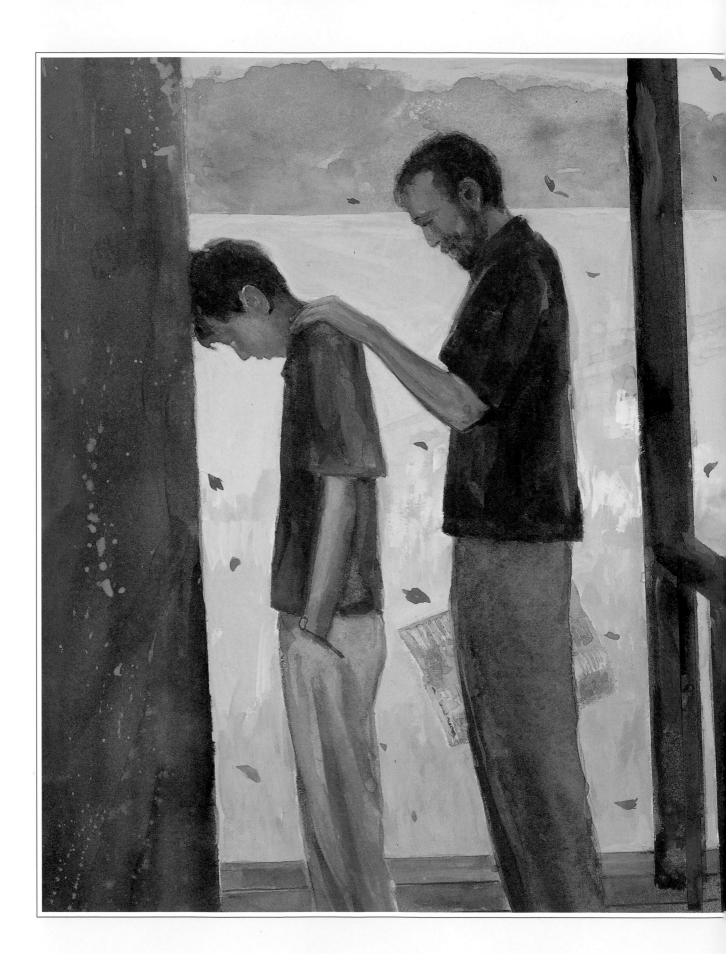

Dearest baby, child of mine
I will kiss you when you fall.

I will love you all your life
Whether you are near or far

And when days are short and cold
Or when winter snows descend

Dearest baby, child of mine
I will love you all your life.

Grow and flourish, dearest child
As you travel down the road

Hold the friend who cannot sleep

Hug the child who cries alone

Kiss the one who starts to fall

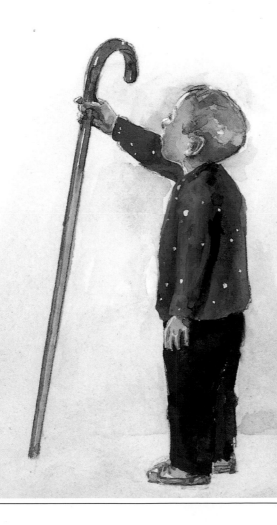

Love and be loved all your life.

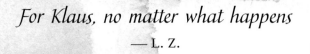

For Klaus, no matter what happens
— L. Z.

For Julianna
— J. M.

Published by Scholastic Press and Arthur A. Levine Books, imprints of Scholastic Inc., *Publishers since 1920.*
SCHOLASTIC and the LANTERN LOGO are trademarks and/or registered trademarks of Scholastic Inc. No part of
this publication may be reproduced, stored in a retrieval system, or transmitted in any form or by any means,
electronic, mechanical, photocopying, recording, or otherwise, without written permission of
the publisher. For information regarding permission, write to Scholastic Inc., Attention:
Permissions Department, 557 Broadway, New York, NY 10012.

LIBRARY OF CONGRESS CATALOGING-IN-PUBLICATION DATA
Zuckerman, Linda.   I will hold you 'til you sleep / by Linda Zuckerman ; illustrated by Jon J Muth. — 1st ed.   p. cm.
Summary: A parent expresses undying love for a child.   ISBN 0-439-43420-3   [1. Parent and child—Fiction. 2. Love—Fiction.]
I. Muth, Jon J, ill. II. Title. III. Title: I will hold you until you sleep.   PZ7.Z78Iaw 2006   [E]—dc22   2005024046

10 9 8 7 6 5 4 3 2   06 07 08 09 10
Printed in Singapore 46

The artwork was created in watercolor and gouache.
The text type was set in 36-point Carmela. Book design by David Saylor
FIRST EDITION, OCTOBER 2006